C000196408

Fishing

Lucas Kavner

A SAMUEL FRENCH ACTING EDITION

SAMUEL FRENCH

FOUNDED 1830

SAMUELFRENCH.COM
SAMUELFRENCH-LONDON.CO.UK

FOR PRODUCTION ENQUIRIES

UNITED STATES AND CANADA
Info@SamuelFrench.com
1-866-598-8449

UNITED KINGDOM AND EUROPE
Plays@SamuelFrench-London.co.uk
020-7255-4302

Each title is subject to availability from Samuel French, depending upon country of performance. Please be aware that *FISH EYE* may not be licensed by Samuel French in your territory. Professional and amateur producers should contact the nearest Samuel French office or licensing partner to verify availability.

MUSIC USE NOTE

Licensees are solely responsible for obtaining formal written permission from copyright owners to use copyrighted music in the performance of this play and are strongly cautioned to do so. If no such permission is obtained by the licensee, then the licensee must use only original music that the licensee owns and controls. Licensees are solely responsible and liable for all music clearances and shall indemnify the copyright owners of the play(s) and their licensing agent, Samuel French, against any costs, expenses, losses and liabilities arising from the use of music by licensees. Please contact the appropriate music licensing authority in your territory for the rights to any incidental music.

IMPORTANT BILLING AND CREDIT REQUIREMENTS

If you have obtained performance rights to this title, please refer to your licensing agreement for important billing and credit requirements.

FISH EYE was first produced by Colt Coeur at HERE Arts Center in New York City on June 2, 2011. The performance was directed by Adrienne Campbell-Holt, with sets by John McDermott, costumes by Jessica Pabst, lighting by Grant Yeager, and sound by Daniel Kluger. The Production Stage Manager was Trisha Henson. The cast was as follows:

MAX . . . . Joe Tippett
ANNA . . . . Betty Gilpin
AVERY . . . . Katya Campbell
JAY . . . . Ato Essandoh

CHARACTERS

MAX – mid to late 20s

ANNA – mid to late 20s

AVERY – mid to late 20s

JAY – late 20s

SETTING

The majority of the stage is Max and Anna's studio apartment in Brooklyn, which can be open to interpretation, design-wise, but must have two entrances/exits, and one front door that can be isolated by light.

Anna's moving boxes could be part of the set; items are packed and unpacked throughout the show.

AUTHOR'S NOTE

A slash (/) indicates that the next character's dialogue should begin.

** indicates a pause, or a shift in tone of some kind.

As the play unfolds, characters can be places you wouldn't expect them to be onstage.

ONE

*(**MAX** and **ANNA** sit, off left, holding beers.)*

(They are isolated by light.)

(A moment as they take each other in for the first time in a while.)

*(Then **ANNA** looks out at something.)*

ANNA. How long has that been there?

MAX. Oh, like a month.

ANNA. It used to be a karate place, right? Like karate classes or jujitsu –

MAX. It was empty for a while.

ANNA. Is the food good?

MAX. It's falafels, you know.

Just, like, Middle Eastern –

ANNA. Mmm.

MAX. Kebobs.

ANNA. Cool.

MAX. Hummus plates.

Pita.

(They look at each other, sort of laugh.)

Fuck, it's…

ANNA. I know, I just want to, like…

MAX. What?

ANNA. Like…

(She makes a gripping gesture.)

MAX. Murder?

ANNA. No, it's just *very*…

Everything comes back like:

(She chops the air.)

MAX. Chops.

ANNA. Yeah.

MAX. I almost sent you an email the other night. Drunk. I never sent it to you. I didn't think it was appropriate and I didn't – I dunno, it didn't –

ANNA. What did it say?

MAX. You know, like, "Go fuck yourself."

ANNA. Oh.

MAX. I'm glad I saved that in drafts. I save a lot of things in drafts.

(They lock eyes again.)

Scooter.

ANNA. *(makes a sound)*

MAX. Sorry.

ANNA. Yeah, don't…

MAX. Sorry.

ANNA. It's OK.

MAX. So.

How many guys are you sleeping with?

ANNA. Max.

MAX. But you're definitely sleeping with someone –

ANNA. Max.

MAX. What?

ANNA. I said I didn't / want to…

MAX. I know, I know.

ANNA. You agreed.

MAX. I know, but seeing you is…

ANNA. I just wanted to see you're OK. And you are.

MAX. I am. I'm great.

ANNA. So am I.

MAX. Really?

ANNA. Yeah, things are good, you know? Things are…

MAX. You look the same.

ANNA. Do I?

MAX. Uh huh.

ANNA. You don't.

MAX. I'm fatter.

ANNA. Yes, that's what I was gonna say.

> (*They stare at each other.*)

MAX. So… I have something.

ANNA. What?

MAX. For you. I have something for you.

ANNA. Uh oh.

MAX. No, it's – this is good. You'll…

> (**MAX** *pulls out a folded-up piece of paper from his pocket and hands it to her.*)

> (**ANNA** *unfolds it and looks at it.*)

ANNA. Oh.
  Wow.

> (*beat*)

MAX. You remember?

> (*beat*)

  That's still how I see you.

> (*A long moment as* **ANNA** *takes it in.*)

> (*Then* **MAX** *stands and the lights shift, revealing the apartment.*)

TWO

*(**AVERY** enters the space.)*

(She grabs a drink from the kitchen.)

AVERY. I can't believe I've reached the point where I'm coming to a game night at your apartment by my*self* and I'm actually OK with it.

MAX. You love us.

AVERY. It's important for you to get out of the house once in a while, see the outside world –

ANNA. It's *cold* out there.

AVERY. Oh Jesus, is that where we're at now?

MAX.	**AVERY**.
It's very cold.	Oh my God.

AVERY. You don't leave the house because it's *cold?*

MAX. I've always tried to stay with the heat.

AVERY. That's a good motto.

MAX. That's the way I've been my whole life, Avery, I'm extremely practical / to a fault.

AVERY. Oh yeah, you've always struck me as *practical.*

MAX. I *feel* practical.

ANNA. I was outside all day on a shoot, it was freezing.

MAX. I was indoors sitting at a computer and crying.

ANNA. You weren't *crying,* / come on –

AVERY. Maxie, how's your job? You, like, never talk about it –

MAX. It sucks dick.

AVERY.	**ANNA**.
Oh, neat.	That's what he always says.

AVERY. Maybe that should indicate something to you, Maxie-pad.

MAX. About what?

AVERY. The fact that you hate your job.

ANNA. He doesn't *hate* his job, he only *says* – Max, tell her that thing about what your boss said last week. About the presentation.

MAX. My boss said I made a very good presentation.

AVERY. Nice.

ANNA. No, come on, that's not all she said, / she said you –

MAX. *(deliberately loud)* My boss said I made a really good presentation and if I kept at it I might become president of the United States.

　　**

ANNA. *(to* AVERY*)* How are the little rich kids?

AVERY. Oh, the – no, I haven't been doing the nannying for a while.

MAX. She's been catering.

AVERY. What? Dude, I'm not *catering,* I'm working at La Sala.

MAX. La Sala?

ANNA. That fancy restaurant? / Isn't that on –

AVERY. Yeah, it's good, I like it –

ANNA. I walked by there last week when we were shooting up by –

MAX. Where's that, like South Brooklyn?

AVERY. Uh, the Upper West Side?

Very close, though.

You could come and visit, that's something friends do.

　　*(*ANNA *opens up the game, starts arranging it.)*

MAX. You're always doing a million things, I can never keep track.

AVERY. What's hard to keep track? I quit my nanny job and now I'm waiting tables at La Sala.

MAX. Do you get discounts?

ANNA.	AVERY.
Crap, we don't have a timer.	I get ten percent off, I think

MAX. That's low.

ANNA. Guys, We don't have a timer.

AVERY. Do you have an hourglass thing from another game?

ANNA. Oooh, I don't know, I can look.

MAX. Just use your phone.

AVERY. How long does it go for, though? / Like how much –

ANNA. I swear I have an hourglass thing somewhere.

MAX. Just use your phone.

ANNA.	**AVERY**.
Calm *down*, I will, but –	What games have hourglasses?

MAX. Ann just use your phone it has a stopwatch thing.

ANNA. How long does it go for, though??

MAX.	**AVERY**.
Like two minutes?	Thirty seconds.

MAX. Thirty *seconds*? What the hell kind of Boggle are you playing?

AVERY. Normal Boggle.

MAX. Crazy Boggle.

ANNA. I know we have an hourglass.

MAX. It's not really important, we can just wing it.

ANNA. It *is* important, if we're gonna play we might as well do it right.

> (**MAX** *takes out his phone, looks up the Boggle rules.*)

> (*And now* **ANNA** *is not there [even though she's still there physically, it's one of those things.]*)

THREE

*(**AVERY** rests her head on **MAX**'s shoulder.)*

(Another time, two years earlier.)

AVERY. She's probably just busy.

MAX. She's not busy, she's ignoring me –

AVERY. Well then what can you possibly do about it on your phone?

MAX. She just became friends with this one guy and I just want to look to see if the, uh, *(distracted)* ...thing...

AVERY. Oh I'm sorry, you trailed off.

MAX. I just want to see if this is the guy Adam said he saw her with, this guy from one of her P.A. jobs or –

AVERY. Her what jobs?

MAX. P.A. jobs, she works on movies.

AVERY. Wow, man, you're having people check *up* on her now? They're like your personal investigators?

MAX. No, not at all, that's –

No, Adam just saw her out with some friends at a bar and he called and told me about it...

(He finds the guy on his phone.)

Paul Abrams.

Fuck Paul Abrams.

*(**AVERY** takes the phone from **MAX**.)*

AVERY. Who is this girl? I've never seen you like this with anyone. Even in college with Erin you didn't get like this.

MAX. That's because I didn't like Erin very much.

AVERY. You guys went out for a year.

MAX. I know and did we ever like each other?

*(**AVERY** thinks about this. **MAX** grabs the phone back.)*

MAX. She should block her photos, it's really weird that I can look at all her photos when I'm not even friends with her.

AVERY. It's weird for her or it's weird for you?

FOUR

(Lights.)

(Now we're back to Boggle.)

(**MAX** *looks up from his phone.)*

MAX. OK, it's three minutes.

AVERY. Oh good! So you weren't right, either, that's a total relief for me.

ANNA. Should I just start it?

AVERY. We have to shake the box first.

MAX. Anna already shook it.

AVERY. Yeah but then we sat around and thought about how long the timer goes for so we all saw the letters.

MAX. That's just – ridiculous, / that's a ridiculous thing to say.

ANNA. I want to shake it again! I love shaking it.

MAX. Why don't we all just shake it together as a family?

ANNA. Oh, hush –

MAX. That way everyone gets a turn.

> (**ANNA** *shakes the Boggle cube. She has trouble getting the letters lined up.)*

OK, are we ready now? I'm gonna start it.

AVERY. You can't look at the cubes.

MAX. I'm not looking at the cubes, / I'm looking at the timer.

AVERY. You *are* looking at the cubes, I'm watching you look at the cubes.

ANNA. This has gone on long enough, OK, just press it.

AVERY. No! Wait…

I have to pee.

MAX. Are you serious?

AVERY. Yeah, I'm sorry, I have to pee. Just cover the cubes.

MAX. This is bullshit, you can't just get up and walk out!

AVERY. You didn't even care about the game five seconds
    ago!
    And you two aren't allowed to fall asleep or be watching
    "West Wing" when I get back.

ANNA. No / promises.

MAX. No promises.

        (**AVERY** *walks off to the bathroom.*)

        (**ANNA** *packs the Boggle back up and puts it in
        the box.*)

        (**ANNA** *puts a phone to her ear, stands.*)

FIVE

(*JAY appears off left with a backpack.*)

(*His energy and enthusiasm are infectious.*)

JAY. Annabelle! Oh man, I'm so sorry I took like eight weeks to get back to you, I was completely... I was in Budapest for this conference and we ended up staying an extra two weeks to try and nail down this Eastern-Hungarian government guy who's trying to get all their buses to run on bio-fuel, but we got all these pat downs from these tiny Magyar men with long beards and it was just a total shit show, I ended up getting my arm caught in a...

(*He stops and looks suddenly to one side.*)

Whoa, holy shit! That guy almost – oh fuck that guy almost got hit by a car on his...

Jesus. No, he's good, he's – Jesus.

(**ANNA** *puts on a big, blue winter jacket.*)

(*She sits with* **MAX** *on the couch, as* **MAX** *starts fiddling with his guitar.*)

Uh, sorry, so, yeah yeah yeah. Video stuff.

I totally want to try and get you something on the next trip, OK? I think it's somewhere...

I don't know, I'll have to ask the planning guy, I just go where they tell me. I'm not sure what our budget is, but you know I love your movies and I only know how to do those star wipe fade things, I'm terrible at that editing stuff, so it'd be great if we could get you onboard, and uh...what am I saying? (*laughs*) I don't know!

But I'll be in New York in two weeks and I'd love to see you! See you and your boy –

Max – see your place, if that's cool.

Miss you, Annabunga!

SIX

(The apartment.)

*(**MAX** finishes playing a song on guitar.)*

ANNA. That's so pretty.

MAX. Yeah, it's not really supposed to be *pretty*, I guess, but yeah that's the kind of stuff I play.

ANNA. I don't know what I was expecting when you said you were going to play me a *song* –

MAX. Something douchey.

ANNA. Yeah.

MAX. You thought I'd just take a shit on the guitar strings.

ANNA. Yes, I thought you would put the guitar on the floor and take a big long shit on it.

*(**MAX** looks hard at **ANNA**.)*

MAX. I used to do that.

ANNA. Oh yeah?

MAX. Yeah, it was part of my dark period. The Brown Period. I can burn you a copy if you want. It was a series of political movements, a dense concept album.

ANNA. You should play a show, have you ever thought about that?

MAX. I don't think I'm a per*former* or anything –

ANNA. Why not?

MAX. Plus I'd need to, like, send some demos out or something – is that how you do it?

ANNA. Yeah, you put your stuff out there.

MAX. I just like messing around.

ANNA. But you're good, you should be sharing your work with people.

MAX. Mmmm…

*(**MAX** tinkers a bit more.)*

ANNA. I'm also really good at guitar.

MAX. Oh yeah?

(**ANNA** *grabs the guitar from* **MAX**.)

(*She sits next to him and tries to play at least one chord.*)

(*She can't quite find it.*)

(**MAX** *is enthralled.*)

MAX. That's the best song I've ever heard.

(*They slowly lean into each other and kiss.*)

(*The guitar is still in the way.*)

MAX. I'm gonna put the guitar down now.

ANNA. Have you ever lived with roommates? I can't imagine not –

(**MAX** *leans in again.*)

Hey, I'm trying to ask you questions about things.

MAX. No, yeah, I know, they're really great.

(*more kissing*)

(**MAX** *starts to take off her jacket.*)

ANNA. No, wait wait wait, I'm leaving this on.

MAX. You're leaving your jacket on.

ANNA. I'm not ready to have sex.

MAX. That's fine, that's totally –

ANNA. I just have to…leave my jacket on.

MAX. That's very weird.

ANNA. It's not weird!

MAX. It's fine that you don't want to have sex, but you're wearing a giant winter jacket.

ANNA. If I take off the jacket I'll have sex with you.

MAX. You will?

(**ANNA** *nods.*)

Just like that?

(*She nods again.*)

So you take off this jacket and that's it. You're fucked.

ANNA. Yeah.

Literally.

MAX. It's your magical abstinence jacket.

ANNA. No, it's just big and bulky and heavy and reminds me that I'm leaving right *now*.

(She stands and moves to the door.)

(She stares at the door.)

(Then she moves back to the couch and sits again.)

MAX. You're back.

(She nods.)

*(**MAX** buries himself in her jacket.)*

ANNA. What are you doing?

MAX. Burrowing.

ANNA. I don't want you in here.

MAX. *(in a weird Dracula voice)* Let me in!

ANNA. Who's that supposed to be?

MAX. I'm like that vampire movie. If you let me in then I'm in here forever –

ANNA. I have to button your head inside.

MAX. Fine, button me, I like it in here.

(A moment with him in her jacket.)

ANNA. OK, I have to gooooo nowwww, / Max.

MAX. You can't.

ANNA. I can.

MAX. Noooooooo.

(She pulls him out. He continues to hold onto her arm.)

ANNA. Call me soon, OK?

MAX. How soon? When? How soon, Anna?! When?!

ANNA. I don't know just call me soon.

MAX. In five minutes.

ANNA. I'll be on the subway.

MAX. Not if you stay here in this house.

ANNA. I just said I'm leaving.

MAX. I know, but what if you *don't*, howsabout that? Howsabouts if you stay.

Stay.

Stay.

Stay.

Stay.

Howabout if you stay.

> (**ANNA** *exits through the kitchen.*)

Stay.

Stay.

Stay.

> (*She grabs a box of her stuff and re-emerges through the front door.*)
>
> (*She begins to move in to* **MAX** *'s apartment.*)
>
> (**MAX** *helps her as…*)

SEVEN

*(**AVERY** appears off right.)*

(She's on the subway, above ground, on the phone.)

AVERY. What? Holy shit, you've only known her like three months!

Well, still, you know, it hasn't been that long, she must really…

Is your stupid apartment big enough? We could barely fit that couch in there when you moved in.

*(in **MAX** voice)* "PUSH THE STUPID THING FORWARD, AVE."

Yeah, that's you. That's my impression of you.

Well, congrats, Maxiepad. I will gladly warm your house. Again.

Yeah, who are Anna's friends, even? I don't think I've ever…

Oh, OK, sure, I'll just bring some girls for her to *know* in the city. That's usually how it works, friendship.

K, should I be playing, like, the voice of reason here? *Because*, because sometimes you do things on principle –

Um, howbout everything you've ever *done*, your job, your *wrestling* in college, working at Applebee's our senior year –

Yeah, that's exactly the same thing! We'd all be going out and you'd be like, "No, I have to work," and we'd be all, "Why is Max working at Applebee's?"

I know, I can barely keep a fish alive, let alone a…

But no, OK, listen, Max, you said all this stuff about Erin don't forget, OK, you do things because you feel like you *have* to, you get obsessed with an *idea* of –

(The lights go darker, she's heading underground.)

Shit, every time I'm on the F, I always –

OK, can we finish this later, though? I think it's... Oh, shit. Yeah, I'm in the tunnel.

Shit.

EIGHT

(Music.)

*(**MAX** sleeps.)*

*(**ANNA**, restless, grabs an old camera from the shelf.)*

(She hasn't used this thing in ages.)

*(She goes to **MAX** and records him as he sleeps.)*

(She gets too close and accidentally stirs him.)

(He wakes up.)

(She keeps the camera trained on him.)

(He does something with his hands.)

*(**ANNA** puts the camera down.)*

(Then she opens the front door…)

NINE

(JAY enters the apartment.)

JAY. I kept getting rerouted everywhere, and then they said there's a sick passenger in another car –

ANNA. They always say that when anything goes wrong on the train, it's really bad karma.

JAY. I didn't know whether to take the Two-Three or what –

ANNA. Oh sorry, I should've told you to take the Q.

> *(MAX moves to the kitchen and starts making snack trays.)*
>
> *(Cheese, crackers, and the like.)*
>
> *(He also grabs a few beers.)*

JAY. It's cool, I kind of miss the subway, like, the smell of the underground or whatever –

ANNA. Yeah, whenever I leave New York I always miss the *smell* of the *subway*.

JAY. I don't know, I guess I just like the *idea* of it. Plus I hate driving.

ANNA. Because you're terrible at it.

JAY. I am. I really suck at driving.

ANNA. Skidding around the mountains in your Dodge *Saturn.*

JAY. Dodge *Stratus* –

ANNA. What? I though it was a Saturn –

JAY. Uh, the 'Stratusphere?'

ANNA. Oh, right right, right – 'Stratusphere.'

JAY. The Stratusphere saw us through two life-threatening blizzards.

ANNA. And that horribly botched attempt to see aurora whatever-its-called –

JAY. Aurora / Borealis.

ANNA. *Borealis*, yes, which apparently only lasts four minutes.

JAY. We just didn't get high enough over the hill.

MAX. *(to himself)* The northern lights.

ANNA. Hey, when did you shave your beard?

JAY. Oh, yeah,

>*(He touches his face.)*

I don't remember, maybe like –

ANNA. All your pictures make you look like a scraggly disaster, I figured you'd still be all *Into The Wild*-ish –

JAY. I had to be in this video promo thing for Climate Core and they made me shave.

ANNA. Bastards.

JAY. *(in Ian McKellen-Gandolf voice)* We must look our best if we are to take on the world –

ANNA. *(same voice)* Ambitions, they are truly an external aim –

MAX. Who is that?

JAY. *(the voice)* Begin your transcendence by first understanding your appearance.

ANNA. *(laughing, to* MAX*)* Oh God, this very – this guy looked like Ian McKellen's scarier uncle, or something, he came and spoke to our class for this career workshop senior year about, like, "coming to terms with your physical self."

JAY. It was called, "Understanding Your Physical Presence."

ANNA. *(to* JAY*)* I think Monica boned that guy when she was working at CSO.

You met Monica, didn't you? At the thing?

>*(*MAX *shakes his head.)*

JAY. Monica: who is having a *real baby* in four months –

ANNA. Two babies! Adam told me she's having *twins*.

JAY. What? Oh no, no, / no –

ANNA. She can't even make *eggs* by herself, remember Montreal, she didn't even know whether you butter the pan –

JAY. Those babies will…die. They're going to die.

(**ANNA** *laughs.* **JAY** *holds up his beer in a toast.*)

JAY. Adulthood.

ANNA. Aaaaaaaaaah.

MAX. We are adults.

(They cheers.)

JAY. Hey, so you and Max – you guys just moved in here, right?

ANNA.	**MAX**.
Like four months ago?	A couple months ago, yeah –

ANNA. This is Max's place from before, I really like it.

JAY. Yeah, it's nice.

(beat)

ANNA. So where you off to next, Captain America, weren't you just in Denmark or something?

JAY. Yeah, I was, uh – Copenhagen for the Climate Core Gas conference thing.

ANNA. *(finds this hilarious)* Gas conference!

JAY. Yup –

ANNA. A bunch of farty environmental activists sitting around...farting.

JAY. That's good, Ann.

MAX. Fart conference.

(short beat)

JAY. Oh, hey, I have key chains for you guys!

(He pulls out two key chains from his bag.)

(Hefty steel Earth balls with gas fumes coming out.)

ANNA. Oooooh.

JAY. These are very high-end, sterling silver.
Or plastic. I'm not sure.

ANNA. I used to collect these.

JAY. Really?

MAX. *(reading from the keychain)* "If you can't stand the heat..."

JAY. Yeah, this whole conference... I can't even...

It was such an amazing, life-changing experience. There are just so many people involved in this movement now, working their asses off, so to be able to get them together in one *place* actually talking and *moti*vating each other and working, and I got to meet Greg Neeling who's basically like the Dutch version of me, the guy does so much work for Climate Core worldwide and to actually sit down with him and talk in *person*, was amazing, since we're always talking on Skype, most of the climate movement is done over *Skype*, you know? / so to be able to –

MAX. *(a little song under his breath)* Goat cheese, goat cheese, gotta have goat cheese.

(the shortest beat)

JAY. What's that?

MAX. Oh, nothing, sorry.

ANNA. No, what'd you say, babe?

MAX. It was really nothing, honestly –

ANNA. *(quieter)* Come on, don't do that, I hate it when / you do that.

MAX. Seriously, it was nothing.

ANNA. Just – what'd you say?

MAX. You're gonna be really embarrassed you made a big deal about this / when I tell you –

ANNA. You're making a bigger deal about it by being weird about telling us –

MAX. OK, I sang, "Goat cheese, goat cheese, gotta have goat cheese."

**

JAY. Nice.

MAX. Yeah, something on the plate had goat cheese in it so I just...

ANNA. OK.

(JAY *laughs, trying to lighten the mood.*)

JAY. Hey, I'm with you, man.

(ANNA *mouths something to* MAX, *privately.*)

(MAX *shakes his head at her.*)

Hey, Max, do you do social media stuff?

MAX. Huh?

JAY. We have a stipend for social networking stuff at Climate Core and Anna said you did some of that at your day job –

MAX. Mmm, sort of, not really social networking –

JAY. You still in that same office?

MAX. Still in the office, yeah. It's not really a "day job," it's pretty much my *job* job, 'cause it's my only source of income.

JAY. What is it you do there, again, isn't it a – ?

MAX. It's an executive search firm, so I mostly – you know, do office stuff. I print and copy shit, I make spreadsheets –

ANNA. No, you're also in charge of –
He's also in charge of all their advertising.

MAX. I'm in charge of their print advertising. Once in a while they post a really, like, shitty ad in a newspaper for their services.

JAY. Well, we always need that kind of help at Climate Core, so I'd be happy to bring you on –

ANNA. That'd be great.

MAX. Yeah, I mean – I can barely stand that stuff at the office, so not sure how much help I'd be.

(*He plays with his silverware, or something else slightly distracting.*)

But uh… I'd definitely be willing to…give it a look.

ANNA. Max is playing slide guitar for this band now.

MAX. I'm not playing "slide guitar" it's – I'm just playing some guitar for them while their other guy – it's just like backup.

JAY. Oh, that's awesome! I didn't know you played music.

ANNA. Max is an incredible guitar player, like kind of country stuff, like Neil Young-ish kind of –

MAX. We're just – you know, we're just fucking around right now –

ANNA. Don't sell it short, babe, they're super serious about it, they even made a little logo for the band, it's this like / wedge of –

MAX. *(just to* **ANNA***)* We didn't make a *logo*, I just drew a stupid thing on Photoshop.

JAY. *(nicely)* Well, you just have to be de*term*ined, man. Like you *should* be making a logo – you should be doing the kinds of things you want to do and make them your focus, right? Like I remember when I started Climate Core and it was like every single piece of advice I got was about how difficult it was going to be to actually get anything *done* –

MAX. No I mean, yeah, I'm gonna keep at it. I have every intention of keeping at it.

JAY. Good, good, cause things are so hard right now, man. In every field.

Everyone's struggling.

Even after we got our initial funding and then the grant from the Clinton Initiative it was like, "What's next?" What can I actually accomplish with this money, you know, how do / we best serve –

MAX. Yeah and then before you know it you're just sucking his cock.

(short beat)

JAY. Whose cock?

MAX. Bill Clinton's cock.

*(***JAY*** nods.)*

*(***ANNA*** looks at* **MAX** *hard.)*

TEN

*(**AVERY** appears off left, she stumbles across the stage on her phone.)*

*(Bar music plays as **JAY** exits the apartment.)*

AVERY. *(loud, drunk)* Because it's my birthday, you shit! You still have a few hours, you have to come.

Because I put it on the day, because Thursday's the new Friday, your job should know that and understand that –

Max. It's my fuckin' birthday. Are you really gonna –

Come on.

Well, what are you doing?

No, no, what are you doing right *now?*

God, I'm gonna hold this against you so hard.

I'm putting five pins in my Max voodoo doll, I'm stabbing you in the face with a pin when I get home, seriously, I'm stabbing you in the eye.

So, you know, if your eye hurts, that's from me. Stabbing it.

(Music from the bar drowns her out and bleeds into.)

ELEVEN

*(**MAX** reads the paper.)*

*(**ANNA** grabs a dreamcatcher from one of the boxes.)*

(She moves to a wall and hammers a nail into it.)

*(**MAX** looks up from his reading.)*

MAX. Hm.

ANNA. What.

MAX. What are you, / uh…

ANNA. I'm just hanging something.

MAX. I know, what is it?

ANNA. It's just a thing.

MAX. What is it, though?

*(**ANNA** holds up the dreamcatcher.)*

Oh, cool.

(beat)

Is that, like, an important thing for you?

ANNA. Is it what?

MAX. No, just – does this have, like, sig*nifi*cance to you?

ANNA. I've had it since I was little, yeah, my mom gave it to me 'cause I had all these nightmares.

MAX. OK.

ANNA. I found it when I was home last week.

*(**MAX** nods, returns to his paper.)*

(But he can't stop staring at the Dreamcatcher.)

Max.

MAX. Yeah?

ANNA. Do you want me to take it down?

MAX. No.

ANNA. I can move it if you want, it's kind of center stage / right here.

MAX. Yeah, I guess – I dunno, maybe you can put it in the kitchen or something?

ANNA. OK.

MAX. Or the bathroom? Don't people usually put Dreamcatchers in the bathroom?

ANNA. I'll put it wherever you want, just tell me where you want me to put it.

MAX. I'm saying I don't care where you put it.

ANNA. Great, then I'm just going to leave it here.

MAX. *(not cool)* Cool, cool.

**

ANNA. OK, you're being extremely… *Max-ish* about this. / Clearly it bothers you.

MAX. Max-ish! That's – no, it doesn't bother me.

ANNA. It does bother you, you did that "Cool, cool" thing that you do that I hate –

MAX. You hate when I say 'cool?'

ANNA. I hate when you say 'cool, cool,' the way you do. You're telling me you don't have anything on any of your walls that means something to you even though it's lame?

MAX. Probably, I don't know.

ANNA. Nothing from your childhood you keep around –

MAX. Um, I still have my camp counselor t-shirt in my closet from when I was a…camp counselor? I don't know, that's / kind of important.

ANNA. I'm asking – no, I'm asking about walls, stuff on dis*play*, you don't keep things that are important?

MAX. I know what you're asking about and I guess I just don't keep stuff. I keep things in my head boxes, you know, I remember things –

ANNA. Your *head* boxes?

MAX. Yeah, I'm not a hoarder, I don't tend to –

ANNA. It doesn't mean you're a *hoarder*.

MAX. I just feel like I'm being reprimanded for just having a decorative opinion –

ANNA. You're not being *reprimanded* I'm just asking you a simple question about the things you choose to keep throughout your life.

MAX. No, you're right, I should definitely keep more stuff, so next time I go home I'll find something stupid in the attic and bring it back here and put it on the wall.

ANNA. That's not what –
It's about caring for things and holding on to them throughout your life.

MAX. How did this become a thing about me?

ANNA. It didn't.

MAX. I just don't want you to put up the Native American bead art in the middle of the room, OK, I didn't ask to be analyzed about the things I hang on to from my fucking *childhood.*

> (ANNA *takes the Dreamcatcher down and hurls it at* MAX.)

> (MAX *acknowledges it for a second. Then goes back to reading.*)

TWELVE

> (**JAY** *enters.*)
>
> *(He sits on the couch.)*
>
> (**MAX** *remains on the bed.*)

JAY. I never thought in a million years you would meet a guy at a party.

ANNA. Why not?

   I'm a hip, fun girl of the city.

JAY. Ohhhh, OK.

ANNA. Where do *you* think I should meet people?

JAY. I don't know, like, an artist's retreat.

ANNA. *An artist's retreat!*

JAY. Yeah, I don't know, I thought you'd go elope with some famous artist man.

ANNA. *(laughs)* Jesus –

JAY. Someone who *whisks* you away with the power of his art.

ANNA. Max whisked me away.

JAY. Cool, that's…

> *(short beat)*

ANNA. What about *you*, Jayface? I bet you meet lots of climate…hoes. Sexy climate hoes –

JAY. Oh yeah, climate hoes never stop…flowin'.

ANNA. "Tell me more, Mr. Barrett, about how *warm* my globe is."

JAY. Mmhm.

ANNA. "I wanna melt your polar ice caps…with my thighs."

JAY. Too easy.

ANNA. "Find me the nearest…snow tiger…and bring him…"

   I lost it.

JAY. I'll put it this way: it's a lot of hotel rooms.

   A lot of weird cities and aggressive…activists.

ANNA. Yeah. You love it.

JAY. I do. It's nice feeling good at the end of my days.

ANNA. You're doing amazing stuff.

JAY. But…it's lonely as hell, too, you know?

Just a lot of: "Hey, I love what you're doing here, Let me tell you about this similar thing that *I'm* doing in the world, I will lay out these points for you, and did I mention we need funding? Here's why you should give me money, thank you very much for your time, here's my card, have a good one – "

ANNA. But you're so good at that.

JAY. I know, but it gets…

ANNA. You miss having a weird film girl around to talk about weird film stuff.

JAY. Yes! Of course I do. I loved that.

ANNA. I don't even know if I can, like…

I haven't made anything in ages.

JAY. Yeah, what's up with that?

ANNA. I've been working, I'm – you know, I'm climbing the *lad*der.

JAY. Alright, but you also need to be making your own stuff, that's the whole point of the work –

ANNA. You only knew me when I made weird shit back in college –

JAY. Yeah, Fucking A, it was weird, it was amazing!

That movie you made for your video art class? With the carrots and celery, that stop motion animation thing with the, like, all the different food fighting each other –

ANNA. Oh, shoot me in my face –

JAY. When the celery commits suicide by drowning himself in the cream cheese?

ANNA. That video was so stupid, Jay, that was like the dumbest thing I've ever done / in my life –

JAY. It *wasn't*, Ann.

Do we need to have a "what color is your parachute" conversation here?

That thing came from the depths of your brilliant brain, and it made people feel something really good and that's important.

ANNA. It wasn't *important*, Jesus, come on –

JAY. It *was*, though.

Why do you say that?

You know it was.

> (**ANNA** *shakes her head and makes a sound, like "Can we stop this conversation?"*)

**

JAY. You should start thinking about grad school.

ANNA. Grad school.

JAY. For film. Or video. Something visual. Have you thought about it?

ANNA. Yeah, sure, I've *thought* about it. I've also thought about finding a job I *like* and / working at it –

JAY. OK, I just – I think you should really think about that. Because right now it seems like you might be selling yourself short.

> (**ANNA** *shoots him a look.*)

I'm just saying –

ANNA. OK, listen, Doctor Future, I'm not selling myself *short*, I'm working on sets, I'm learning all the stuff first hand, and I want to be in the city.

JAY. *("whatever")* OK.

ANNA. What?

> *(beat)*

JAY. When you look at yourself and where you want to be in five years, do you see yourself doing something creative?

ANNA. Yeah, of course I do. Of course I want to be making things. / That's why I'm –

JAY. And does Max inspire you to want to do that? Does he make you feel something –

ANNA. Definitely, yeah, you know *love* is very...

JAY. Does he make you feel something *real?*

ANNA. Ugh, for fuck's sake, yes, it's super major real.

JAY. No, I just mean does he –

ANNA. I love Max, OK, this isn't about him. And how are you ever able to define why you're with somebody? You're not. There are qualities in him that I love, just as there were qualities in you that I loved, that I still love.

**

Max makes me laugh. All the time. You never made me laugh.

JAY. What? Yes, I did!

ANNA. We laugh now at things, but back then – we were very serious together, you and me. A very *serious* couple.

JAY. We were driven. That's not a bad thing.

ANNA. Max is driven.

JAY. Awesome, that's –

ANNA. And we love each other.

JAY. Good, that's...yeah, that's what counts.

ANNA. Yeah.

> *(They drink wine.)*

> (**JAY** *checks his watch.*)

JAY. OK. I'm gonna go crash with Adam, I think.

ANNA. OK.

JAY. Unless it's cool if I stay on the couch?

> (**ANNA** *makes a sound*)

> (**JAY** *nods.*)

ANNA. Max is – you know...

JAY. Where is he again?

ANNA. He's home in Ohio, his dad's kinda sick.

JAY. Oh, that sucks.

ANNA. I care about what you *think*, Jay.

> (**MAX** *goes and grabs his guitar. Then he sits back down on the bed.*)

JAY. Yeah, I just want you to…

ANNA. I know, it's hard, though. 'Cause now I'm…

> (*She gestures to the apartment, to her life.*)

JAY. Just watch *Carrots and Celery*, that'll refresh you.

ANNA. I don't even have a copy of that stupid thing.

JAY. That's a tragedy.

> (**ANNA** *smiles. Fidgets.*)

OK, well…

> (*They stand.*)

> (*Maybe some awkward handshake or something.*)

> (*Then they hug for a long moment.*)

ANNA. (*like an old New York Jew*) Gawd, you're so tall.

> (**MAX** *starts fiddling with his guitar on the bed.*)

> (**ANNA** *stays holding* **JAY**.)

> (*They stay like that for a bit, in some sort of weird holding pattern.*)

> (*Finally,* **ANNA** *breaks off and* **JAY** *exits.*)

THIRTEEN

A Montage

(**MAX** *gets out of bed.*)

(*He's excited.*)

(*He goes to the stereo and turns on a song.*)

(*Something a bit overwhelming and mildly ironic, in the style of "The Final Countdown."**)

(*He waits for* **ANNA,** *who emerges from the bathroom in very little clothing.*)

(**MAX** *is enthralled, and embarrassed.* **ANNA** *listens to the song a moment.*)

ANNA. Are you serious?

MAX. I don't… God, I'm such an asshole.

ANNA. Yeah, I…

MAX. You look…

ANNA. I think we were on two different pages –

MAX. No, you…

        (**MAX** *moves to her and kisses her.*)

        (**ANNA** *and* **MAX** *stumble towards the bed.*)

ANNA. Oh, Jesus, I really like you touching that part of my back.

MAX. Which?

ANNA. Just remember where you're touching right now.

MAX. OK, I mean, I / can't –

ANNA. Just remember it, it was nice.

MAX. OK, but I'm not sure I can / get it exactly –

---

*The publisher recommends that the licensee creates an original composition that stays true to the author's intent.

ANNA. You can, Scooter, you can remember.

> *(They shift positions. This is another time now.)*

Wait, stay there –

MAX. I'm done, / I'm done –

ANNA. I know, but just *stay*.

> *(They stay in that position for a long moment.)*

MAX. Are you trying to / finish or – ?

ANNA. Just shut up.

> *(shift)*

> *(They break off of each other on the bed.)*

> *(**ANNA** spits some hair out of her mouth.)*

> *(They splay out, a little catatonic.)*

How many times do you think we've had sex?

MAX. What, like total?

ANNA. Yeah.

MAX. I don't know. Two years? So, like…four hundred and six.

ANNA. Wow, that many?

MAX. Three hundred and ninety five.

ANNA. That's only eleven less than the other one you guessed.

MAX. Is that more or less than you'd say?

ANNA. I guess I'd say…yeah, about that. Wow. That's a lot.

> *(shift)*

FOURTEEN

> (**AVERY** *enters the apartment from the bathroom,
> in a bra.*)
>
> (**ANNA** *gets out of bed, puts on her clothes and exits
> to the kitchen.*)
>
> (**AVERY** *stares at* **MAX**, *who is trying to distract
> himself with something.*)

AVERY. So. Yeah. I'm gonna go.

> (*She doesn't go. She stares at* **MAX**.)

Oh, man.

MAX. What?

AVERY. Fuckin – "What?"

> (*She laughs. Then stops.*)
>
> (*They search the bed for* **AVERY**'s *shirt.*)
>
> (**MAX** *finds it buried under the sheets.*)

MAX. Here.

Do you want a beer, or…?

AVERY. I think we need to figure out what we've been
doing here.

MAX. We've been having sex with each other.

Do we need to…

AVERY. What?

MAX. I don't know. Like – have a conversation about it?

> (*Dumbfounded,* **AVERY** *puts her shirt on.*)
>
> (**MAX** *looks at her, realizing he just said the wrong
> thing. Hating himself.*)

AVERY. Do you know how many…

Through the course of my life, do you…

> (*beat*)

AVERY. I mean, you don't even *touch* me afterwards, Max, you get up and fuckin clean yourself off.

MAX. I'm sorry.

AVERY. Nah, you're never…

Fuck it.

MAX. No, just say.

AVERY. You know what I *feel* about you.

MAX. I don't.

AVERY. Come on, man, that night with the chocolate milk?

>   (**AVERY** *finishes getting dressed.*)

MAX. Are you gonna tell Anna?

AVERY. *(laughs)* I don't know. Yeah, I probably should.

MAX. What would you…

I mean – what, you're just gonna send her an *email* in California?

AVERY. I don't know – I don't know what I'm going to *do*, Max, what are *you* going to do?

MAX. She kissed someone last month.

AVERY. Well. You fucked me this month.

>   (**AVERY** *grabs* **ANNA**'s *winter coat, from before.*)

>   (*The blue one. From the guitar scene.*)

>   (**MAX** *can't believe it.*)

MAX. What is that?

AVERY. What?

MAX. What's that jacket?

>   (**AVERY** *shakes her head*)

MAX. Have you always had it?

AVERY. No, Max. It was a gift.

>   (*She waits.*)

You can't even walk me out?

>   (**MAX** *stays on the bed.*)

>   (*The light onstage opens up to include* **ANNA**.)

FIFTEEN

(ANNA *digs through a moving box. She holds up a*
brochure she finds.)

ANNA. Hey, remember this? JELLYFISH!

MAX. *(to* ANNA*)* What?

ANNA.   AVERY.
  JELLYFISH! That's all it   I don't think I can be
  says on the thing –   your friend anymore.

MAX. What?

ANNA. JELLYFISH.

MAX. Oh yeah, that aquarium upstate or wherever it was?

AVERY. Do you hear me?

MAX. Yeah.

(*With one last look to* MAX, AVERY *exits – ruined.*)

ANNA. You were an asshole to me that day.

MAX. What? No, I wasn't.

ANNA. You yelled at me because I saved us seats on
  MetroNorth that were backwards and you said you
  would get *train-sick*.

MAX. I didn't *yell* at you, I think we argued about the
  seating –

ANNA. No, you totally did, you actually yelled at me. You
  screamed, you don't remember that?

MAX. I just remember the jellyfish.

ANNA. So many jellyfish.

MAX. Yeah, I don't remember the other stuff. The arguing
  and all that.

(*He drops the brochure back in the box and
approaches* ANNA *on the ground, wraps his arms
around her.*)

It's almost two.

ANNA. Shit, is it really?

MAX. You have to go in less than three hours.

ANNA. What? My flight's not 'til 9:30 –

MAX. Anna, your flight's at 7:05 –

ANNA. What? No way, it's –

MAX. I've looked at the thing like seventeen million times, Scooter, your flight's at 7:05 a.m.

ANNA. Yikes, that's early.

MAX. I told you to get the later flight.

ANNA. Well, I thought I had *booked* the later flight, so it wasn't exactly…

(**MAX** *takes* **JAY***'s keychain out of one of the boxes.*)

(*She laughs. Throws it back in.*)

MAX. Are we gonna have sex tonight, at least?

ANNA. Um.

MAX. I'm serious.

ANNA. I know, it's just – prepare me a little for –

MAX. Are we?

ANNA. I didn't think about it, to be honest.

MAX. Oh yeah? Didn't cross your mind a li'l bit?

ANNA. It – yeah, I mean it did *generally*, but I'm thinking of lots of other things…

MAX. I don't think it's a crazy thing to ask –

ANNA. I know, I know, we should.

MAX. We *should*.

ANNA. I don't know, I'm just…

I don't know.

MAX. You don't know, you don't know, you don't know! The Anna story.

(**MAX** *sits on the edge of the bed.*)

(*He puts his head in his hands.*)

Man, I…

ANNA. Yeah.

MAX. This really…

ANNA. I know.

MAX. Come here.

> (**ANNA** *moves over to* **MAX**.)
>
> (*She climbs on top of him slowly.*)
>
> (*And they just lay there for a moment.*)
>
> (*He kisses her.*)
>
> (*It gets a little bit heavier and he tries to take off her shirt.*)
>
> (**ANNA** *retreats.*)

ANNA. Aaaaaah.

MAX. What?

ANNA. I don't know, / I don't *know* –

MAX. It's been three years, I think it's time I got to second base –

ANNA. It's too much tonight, you know, it just feels too –

MAX. It's not too much! It's your last night, I want to sleep with you.

> (*He kisses her, tries to take off her shirt again, But she doesn't let him.*)

ANNA. No, I'm – sorry, I'm just not feeling it.

MAX. Fuck you.

ANNA. What?

MAX. Just fuck you. What the *fuck*?

ANNA. Can't we just lie here?

MAX. No.

ANNA. Please.

MAX. No, that's not what I want to do.

ANNA. Just lie here with me.

MAX. No, that's all we've been doing the last week.

ANNA. Because that's what I need from you now.

MAX. I need stuff from you, too!

ANNA. I know, I know, just...shhhhhhh.
Come on, please.

Just lie here.
OK?
Please.

>(**ANNA** *lies down next to* **MAX** *and closes her eyes.*)

>(*After a moment,* **MAX**, *restless, gets up and heads out through the kitchen.*)

>(**ANNA** *sleeps.*)

SIXTEEN

(**MAX** *and* **AVERY** *enter through the front door,
dressed in "going out" clothes.* **ANNA** *is still asleep
in bed.*)

(*They talk in an elevated whisper.*)

AVERY. Sure it's OK that we're here?

MAX. Yeah, it's my house.

AVERY. But she's sleeping.

MAX. We're being quiet.

AVERY. Yeah but we're drunk so I could yell by accident.
And I maybe think I'm gonna puke a little?

MAX. Do you want some chocolate milk?

AVERY. What?

MAX. (*louder*) Do you want some chocolate milk?!

AVERY. (*laughs, quiet*) Shhhhh!

MAX. Was that loud?

　　　　(**AVERY** *nods, laughing.*)

Do you want some?

AVERY. You're making chocolate milk, what are you *seven?*

MAX. I wanted some all day.

　　　　(**AVERY** *slides down along the wall.*)

　　　　(**MAX** *makes chocolate milk.*)

How much chocolate do / you like in it?

AVERY. Ugh, I can't feel my *mouth.*

MAX. Ave, how much chocolate do you want in it?

AVERY. My whole mouth is…

MAX. What's wrong with you?

AVERY. I'm just really…

　　　　(**AVERY** *tries to stand, but fails.*)

　　　　(**MAX** *goes to her and props her up.*)

MAX. I didn't think you drank that much.

AVERY. That is where you are wrong, Captain Maxton. Capta-Max.

MAX. You can stay on the couch.

Ave?

Do you want to crash on the couch?

AVERY. I want chocolate milk.

MAX. Ave, let me – here.

>（**MAX** *picks* **AVERY** *up and carries her to the couch.*)

>(*He sets her down, and covers her with a blanket.*)

>(*He tries to go back to the kitchen but* **AVERY** *grabs his arm.*)

AVERY. You're a forever, you know?

MAX. Oh yeah?

AVERY. No, no, in my life, I mean, you're one of the only forever people. You and my friend Gigi from kindergarten.

MAX. Thanks.

AVERY. No fuckin' – *seriously*, you don't ever listen to me because you're a guy and you can't stop that about yourself, but I'm always here for you, because I'm just… you're always there for me and I'm always here for you.

MAX. I know, Ave.

AVERY. What about the camping trip?

Right?

Before that last thing at school we went on, remember what I said to you?

>（**MAX** *nods.*)

I have that photo with you.

MAX. What photo?

AVERY. From the…with the hat?

That's nice to remember.

>(*She kisses him suddenly.*)

MAX. Woah, what the fuck?

AVERY. *(oops)* No, nothing!

>   *(She flops back down on the couch, looks away.)*

MAX. Don't do that.

AVERY. What?

MAX.	**AVERY.**
You're so drunk.	I didn't do it!

MAX. I should get you a cab, probably.

AVERY. No no no don't do that, I'm good, I'm totally good, I'm staying.
See? I'm asleep.

>   *(She curls up and closes her eyes.)*

See?

>   (**MAX** *goes and slides into bed with* **ANNA.** *He holds her tightly.)*

>   (**AVERY** *stays awake a moment, eyes wide open.)*

>   *(She looks out at us.)*

SEVENTEEN

(**JAY** *enters and heads to the kitchen.*)

(*He takes a quiche out of the oven.*)

(**MAX** *moves to the couch and futzes with his computer.*)

JAY. Success!

ANNA. Does it look good?

JAY. Yeah, it's definitely, like, very aesthetically…
   Here, look.

(*He touches the pan and burns his hand.*)

Oh, shit! Ass!

ANNA. (*laughing*) Dude! You OK?

JAY. I got too excited.

ANNA. We worked far too hard on this for you to mess it up at the end here.
   Max, will you get the table ready?

MAX. (*from his computer*) Yeah, just a sec.

ANNA. We're gonna eat in a minute, can you just grab some forks and stuff?

MAX. I just have to finish this thing.

(**ANNA** *waits a moment to see if he'll move.*)

ANNA. Max?

(*They look at each other.*)

(*Realizing* **MAX** *isn't going to move,* **ANNA** *heads to the cutlery drawer.*)

MAX. No, wait, / I'll get it.

ANNA. It's OK.

JAY. Here, lemme help you.

ANNA. Will you grab the salad bowl, actually?

(*They set the table together.* **MAX** *stays on the couch.*)

JAY. Damn, this looks good, too. Good salad work.

ANNA. You used to give me so much shit for buying salad dressing.

JAY. Yeah, 'cause it's four bucks cheaper to make it yourself and you're using the exact same ingredients.

ANNA. Blah blah blah blah environment blah.

(She holds up the candle on the table.)

Candle or no candle?

JAY. Is it scented?

ANNA. Oh shit! I totally forgot your weird thing with scented candles –

JAY. No, it was just a thing about *smells*, like about mixing smells.

ANNA. Oh yeah, what was that weird gas station on the way to Montreal – ?

JAY. It was a gas station with a Hungarian bakery inside.

ANNA. Right, of course.

JAY. The combination of, like, fuel and *pie* –

ANNA. OK, so this candle will too much stimul*ation* for you / is what you're saying –

JAY. Yeah that's – that's exactly what I'm saying.

(MAX stands, shuts his computer, and walks to the table.)

Hey, so when do you leave?

ANNA. Huh?

JAY. For California, isn't it soon?

ANNA. Oh. *(looks at MAX, suddenly more aware)* August tenth, I think, I'm heading out –

JAY. Wow, three months.

ANNA. I guess, yeah.

JAY. You're gonna love it so much, Ann –

ANNA. Yeah, I can't – it's unbelievable. I'm really...

Do you want wine or beer?

JAY. Beer's good. How did you end up picking USC over Columbia, did they give you more money?

(**MAX** *stares at* **ANNA***, hard.*)

ANNA. *(short beat)* Um, yeah, they ended up, uh…
USC is just a better program, honestly.

JAY. That's where Spielberg went, right?

MAX. You got into Columbia?

ANNA. Yeah, babe, I told you that.

MAX. No you didn't.

(*a long silence*)

JAY. But USC is like the best program in the country, right?

ANNA. Yeah.

JAY. Yeah, plus then you get to be connected in L.A afterwards, which is perfect.

ANNA. Yeah, the chance to have that community, / that was mostly what –

MAX. Do you want to use the placemats?

ANNA. Hm?

MAX. The placemats.

ANNA. Sure! Set 'em up.

(**MAX** *goes to the kitchen and grabs blue placemats.*)

(*He drops them on the table and starts setting them up.*)

JAY. You're gonna eat so many In-N-Out burgers.

ANNA. That's what I'm told.

JAY. For breakfast. Just pounding burgers for breakfast.

ANNA. Ha, OK, I gotta run to the bathroom real fast and then we'll eat, yeah?

JAY. Cool.

ANNA. Don't move the candle!

JAY. *(in Ian McKellan voice)* The only thing I will move is the body I possess.

(**ANNA** *exits to the bathroom, leaving* **MAX** *and* **JAY** *alone.*)

(*a long moment*)

(*In silence,* **MAX** *sets up napkins on the table.*)

(**JAY** *plays on his phone, trying to be invisible.*)

(*Finally* **MAX** *sits down and stares at* **JAY**.)

MAX. Who are you texting?

JAY. Ah, nothing, just a little...thing here.

MAX. Cool, cool.

　　　(short beat)

This looks good.

JAY. Yeah, man, thanks for letting us cook here.

MAX. Well, I didn't really have a choice.

JAY. *(laughs)*

　　**

MAX. I read your e-mails sometimes.

JAY. Hm?

MAX. To Anna.

I read your e-mails.

　　　(beat)

JAY. Wow, OK, you...read her *e-mails. (laughs)* That's /
pretty –

MAX. She leaves her email open on the computer
sometimes and it's impossible for me not to look at
them, just 'cause...um...

But, you need to stop, OK?

JAY. I'm sorry?

MAX. You need to stop.

JAY. Stop what?

MAX. Writing her those e-mails.

JAY. Max, I'm not sure you're –

MAX. No, come on, you write her these long, flowery
fucking emails about how *talented* she is, how you miss
her creative *mind*, how she should be following her
*pass*ion because she has so much to *offer* –

JAY. *(very diplomatic)* Hey, come on, man, let's not –
Let's not talk about this here, OK? I'm in town for
another couple days, let's meet tomorrow, I'll buy you
a beer –

MAX. No, you just need to stop writing her, OK? You already
got her to leave, what else / do you want?

JAY. I didn't get her to leave, man, she wants to go to school
out there to do what she wants to do and she *should.*

MAX. No, no, fuck, that's not – it wasn't a *thing* before…
I mean you just *swoop* in and…
Like, some people have to *work*, OK, and *live* – you
know, this is, this is a *life* we have, and she's…

> *(Frustrated,* **MAX** *retreats into himself.)*

> *(***JAY*** just watches him a moment.)*

JAY. Why don't you just go to California with her?

MAX. 'Cause she didn't ask me to.

> *(a brief silence)*

> *(Then* **ANNA** *re-enters from the bathroom. Clearly
> she's been listening.)*

> *(She takes in the weird air for a moment.)*

ANNA. Max, do we still have that bourbon?

MAX. What?

ANNA. That bottle of that fancy bourbon you bought last
month. Did we drink it?

MAX. No, we have more.

> *(***ANNA*** moves to the kitchen.* **JAY** *follows her out.)*

EIGHTEEN

*(**MAX** crumples in a chair, head in his hands.)*

*(**AVERY** enters and stands or sits next to him, rubbing his back.)*

AVERY. We should take a walk, I think.

Maxie.

Let's go for a walk or somewhere, OK?

*(**MAX** doesn't move.)*

I should buy my ticket back home for this weekend. I don't know if I can…

Yeah, I guess I'll head into Cleveland instead of – that probably makes more sense, right?

(beat)

Uh, is the funeral Saturday or Sunday?

Maxie?

MAX. Um.

AVERY. I bet it's gonna be packed. Your dad knew everyone, there's gonna be tons of people there, you're gonna have to see, like – God, you'll probably have to see everyone from high school…

I'm sure everyone's gonna want to be there.

I can't wait to see your mom, she's always so good in these situations, you know, such a warm…

(wrong thing to say)

You talked to him so much, you know, those last few months, you got to say goodbye and that's so important because, like…that's the kind of thing you'll think about and be really – you'll be so *happy* you got to do that.

*(**MAX** stands.)*

Do you want me to call a few people for you? Let me call our friends, who can I call?

MAX. Um…

AVERY. I can do whatever –

MAX. I need to, like write a few things before you –

AVERY.	**MAX**.
OK, let me help you –	Yeah, I'd just rather –

AVERY. Whatever you need.

MAX. I would just rather you… / just can you –

AVERY. I can leave if you want –

MAX. No, you don't have to leave, I just – I don't know what I need from you right now, I have a million things to do, so can we just –

AVERY. That's fine, / that's totally fine –

MAX. Am I *allowed* to do that?
Am I allowed to…

>   *(And then* **ANNA** *comes through the front door.)*
>
>   *(She immediately drops her stuff on the ground and runs to* **MAX**.*)*
>
>   *(They embrace.)*
>
>   *(***MAX*** *cries in her arms.)*
>
>   *(***AVERY*** *backs up.)*

ANNA. Oh, sweetheart.

>   *(She kisses him on the forehead and holds him.)*
>
>   *(***AVERY*** *just watches them for a moment before exiting.)*

NINETEEN

(MAX and ANNA break away from each other.)

(ANNA goes back to packing.)

(MAX plays a song on guitar that he's been working on.)

(He very, very quietly begins to sing a melody.)

(It's nice.)

(ANNA looks at him, smiles.)

ANNA. I hear that.

(MAX stops singing, but keeps playing.)

No, keep singing!

(MAX doesn't.)

What was that song?

MAX. Just something I'm messing with.

ANNA. I really like it.
Will you – *(realizing she keeps disturbing him)*
Sorry.

(MAX stops playing again.)

Will you play a show before I go?

MAX. *(snotty British singer voice)* No shows, can't let these things out of the cages.

ANNA. Seriously.

MAX. *(British voice)* Every song is a gift for me ears.

ANNA. Come on.

MAX. I'll play a show.
If you stay.

(They share a look.)

(MAX smiles.)

(ANNA doesn't.)

(He goes back to playing.)

TWENTY

(**ANNA** *empties out one of the other boxes onto the floor.*)

(*She sorts through it as* **AVERY** *enters and begins perusing* **ANNA***'s stuff.*)

AVERY. What about your sweaters, can I have those?

ANNA. You want my *sweaters*? Like as a whole?

AVERY. Yeah, totally, I love your sweaters, you have great sweaters.

ANNA. I mean – look in the toss box, I think there's a few in there.

(**AVERY** *goes to the "toss box."*)

AVERY. Yeah, this one's OK. What about that awesome one with the pink patches?

ANNA. Which?

AVERY. The pink – or orange. The arm patch things.

ANNA. Oh, I love that one. I can't give you that one.

AVERY. But it's like 80 degrees every day over there. It's the sunshine city.

ANNA. That's Miami.

AVERY. Oh, what's L.A.?

ANNA. The City of Angels.

AVERY. Isn't California the Sunshine State?

ANNA. I think that's Florida?

AVERY. Huh.

ANNA. I don't know anymore. I'm very confused.

AVERY. This is the kind of stuff you need to learn before you go. You also need to know the state bird. They test you at the border on that kind of stuff.

(**AVERY** *looks through the box.*)

(*She finds a DVD –* Carrots and Celery *– a gift from* **JAY** *– in the toss box.*)

What's *Carrots and Celery*?

ANNA. Oh, nothing.

    (**AVERY** *reads from a note on the box.*)

AVERY. "Just wanted to remind you of –"

ANNA. I'm taking that.

AVERY. OK, So no-go on the pink sweater, then?

ANNA. No! Quit tryin' to steal from me, yo.

AVERY. I'm just trying to save you packing space, *Scooter*.

    (*beat*)

ANNA. Oh, wow. Bustin' that out, are ya?

AVERY. Sorry.

ANNA. Oh, no, it's – I've just never heard anyone…

AVERY. I always hear Max call you that.

ANNA. Yeah.

AVERY. What is it?

ANNA. I don't know, it's just a dumb name, there's no reason for it.

AVERY. It doesn't mean anything?

ANNA. No. It's just a stupid thing we call each other. There's no reason.

Oh! Wait, actually, you know what you can take?

    (*She goes to a closet and takes out her blue winter coat.*)

    (*She tosses it to* **AVERY**.)

Here.

AVERY. What? No, this is your nice jacket –

ANNA. I know, but it's huge and bulky and I don't want to put it in the box I'm shipping.

AVERY. *I love* this jacket.

ANNA. And I want you to have it.

AVERY. Yeah, OK.

    (**AVERY** *holds it up.*)

    (*She puts it on.*)

ANNA. Nice.

AVERY. Mmmmm, I look good in this.

ANNA. Don't push it, now.

> (beat)

AVERY. I'm glad I got to know you a little.

ANNA. Oh, I gave you my jacket and you finally like me.

AVERY. What? Fuck that, no, I always liked you.

ANNA. You didn't, but that's cool.

AVERY. I'm just jealous of your whole…

ANNA. What?

AVERY. Just your whole…thing. Your whole you.

ANNA. Shut up, you're not jealous of me.

AVERY. No, I'm just jealous of your clothes.

And hair.

And…torso.

ANNA. Well, you can take my pants, I was just going to offer them to you –

AVERY. You're really this beautiful thing.

> (short beat)

ANNA. Hm.

> (**MAX** enters the apartment in his work clothes.)

> (He drops his bag on the floor and heads to the fridge for a snack.)

AVERY. Why are you leaving, really?

ANNA. Um.

AVERY. You could've stayed in the city if you wanted.

ANNA. Yeah, I don't know, I've been here five years, I wanted something different.

AVERY. Then why don't you bring him with you?

ANNA. Uh…

Can I have my jacket back now?

AVERY. No, sorry, I shouldn't be…

I think you've made him happy, you know, he *lives* for
you. I'm just curious why he's not coming with you.

ANNA. *(taking this hard)* I mean, people have to try things
if they...

You know, if they want to become the best person they
can be.

AVERY. Huh.

> (**MAX** *prepares a bagel and cream cheese.*)

I have such a specific memory of sitting with him there.
And he's just going through all your pictures – like,
you'd met him like a few weeks earlier – and he's just
like completely ob*sessed*, you know, he can't think of
anything else.

Like you were *it*, you were everything.

ANNA. I was obsessed with him, too, I talked about him to
everyone.

AVERY. But not like this. He was basically stalking you.

> (**ANNA** *nods, looks at* **MAX** *who moves to the
> kitchen table and eats his bagel.*)

You're gonna eat a lot of In-N-Out burgers.

ANNA. Yeah, I've heard that.

AVERY. Palm trees.

> (**ANNA** *goes back to packing.*)

ANNA. "You're really this beautiful thing."

AVERY. You are.

> (*They look at each other.*)

TWENTY-ONE

(**MAX** *in the kitchen.*)

(*He continues prepping his snack.*)

MAX. I asked off for next Friday so we can spend an extra day upstate if we want.

They're taking a sick day from me, though, which – you know, I was like: "Just take a *vacation* day, it's part of my vac*ation*," but the HR lady just told me to take a sick day.

ANNA. Yeah, that's…

MAX. Hey, do I have something in my teeth?

(**AVERY** *takes the jacket and exits.*)

ANNA. What?

MAX. I've been playing with something in my teeth all day but I'm not actually sure –

(*She looks in his mouth.*)

There, do you see it?

ANNA. Move your tongue.

(*She looks.*)

I don't see anything.

MAX. What's *that*, though? It feels thick.

ANNA. I'm looking and I don't see anything. I see teeth.

(*She moves to the couch.* **MAX** *eats.*)

MAX. Hey. Did you pick up my computer?

ANNA. Hm?

MAX. My computer, I texted you this morning.

(*She didn't.*)

ANNA. Oh, uh…

MAX. Ahhhhhhh, cock.

ANNA. I'm sorry, I got completely waylaid –

MAX. It's been sitting there for two days, the geniuses probably came all over it.

ANNA. I know, I'm really sorry. I suck.

MAX. Alright. I should probably…

ANNA.	MAX.
Can I talk to you about something, though?	Shit, I should've done that on my way home.

> *(He goes to the dresser and changes out of his work clothes. ANNA watches him.)*

ANNA. *(off the cuff)* Did you watch the final version of my short?

MAX. Hm?

ANNA. The final cut of *Flutes*, Andy sent the edited link today and I e-mailed it to you.

MAX. Oh yeah, the thing with the superhero guy?

ANNA. Yeah, I mean –

Yeah. What did you think of the changes?

MAX. I liked it.

ANNA. What about the changes?

MAX. Yeah, I liked them. I really liked what you changed.

ANNA. It's completely color-corrected and I re-organized the ending, plus the titles are a little more, like –

MAX. Yeah, no, it's good. The color looks really good.

ANNA. I spent a lot of time on it.

MAX. I know, and it looks really good.

> *(ANNA takes a moment and considers.)*

> *(It's clear her head is spinning.)*

ANNA. I'm gonna use it to apply for school, I think.

MAX. Use what?

ANNA. That short. To apply for film school. I've been working here for a while and I'm starting to feel pretty stagnant as a P.A. and I'd like to –

MAX. Yeah, you should.

ANNA. You think so?

MAX. Yeah, you'll totally get in.

ANNA. I'd have to, like, apply for stuff out of the city, too…
    (short beat)

Like out of New York.

MAX. Like where?

ANNA. Like California, maybe Austin, couple other places with good programs.

MAX. Yeah, I mean…yeah. I've always wanted to go to Austin.

ANNA. Yeah.
    **

MAX. Of course I'd rather you didn't go anywhere, since we live together and I plan on spending the rest of my life with you.

ANNA. What?

MAX. I plan on spending the rest of my / life with you.

ANNA. I know, I heard, it's just – God, you make these grand statements like out of nowhere.

MAX. I would just rather you didn't leave, can I say that?

ANNA. I would rather I didn't either, Scooter. I don't want to leave –

MAX. That should probably be a priority.
    (He finishes dressing and grabs his bag.)

Do you need anything from the world?

ANNA. Wait, I don't want to leave things like this, I think we should –

MAX. Am I a priority for you?

ANNA. Yes.

What? Of course.

MAX. But I'm not first.

ANNA. *(hesitates ever so slightly)* I don't…have a list of priorities –

MAX. You're first on my list.

ANNA. OK.

MAX. You're first.
    *(**MAX** exits, leaving **ANNA** behind.)*

TWENTY-TWO

(**AVERY** *appears off left.*)

AVERY. I don't know why I'm calling you. It's been, Jesus, like half a year or something insane.

God. Something crazy. Um, what was I gonna...?

Oh, you'll be proud of me, I left the restaurant and I finally got a teaching job. I'm teaching third grade in Jersey City.

Molding the future Snookies of America, like I always... planned. So.

Um.

The internet told me you...

(*A fire truck passes, siren blaring. She waits.*)

Sorry... Uh, sorry...

(*silence*)

So listen, I kind of hate you for everything. I always will, I think. But I hope you and Anna have figured some shit out and you're in a good place with yourself in the world. I just want to know you're OK. Generally.

I'm always here, you know?

That's what's so fucked up.

I'll always just see you in that *way*, you know, in that stupid green hat from that night in Grafton when you were all...

But just know that.

Someone's always here.

(*She hangs up. We linger on her a moment.*)

TWENTY-THREE

(**ANNA** *is asleep on the couch.*)

(**MAX** *is asleep on the bed.*)

(*A moment, and suddenly* **MAX** *shoots up. He checks the clock.*)

MAX. Holy fuck.

(*He scrambles up, sees* **ANNA**, *goes to her to wake her up.*)

Hey, hey.

(*He shakes her.*)

Hey, you gotta go. You gotta go now, like now –

ANNA. *(waking up)* Huh? How is the salaverse… *(nondescript sleep nonsense)*

MAX. You gotta go, it's already like 5:30, you gotta go like now now now.

ANNA. No, 'cause it's not gonna be / over there –

MAX. Did you not set your alarm? Why were you sleeping on the couch?

ANNA. I don't know what happened, / I must've –

MAX. OK, Ann, you gotta like zip all your suitcases and throw on some clothes, I'll ship you whatever you need, OK?

ANNA. I'm not even done packing, I just fell asleep –

MAX.	ANNA.
It's OK, I'll just ship you the rest of your stuff, alright?	What time is it?

ANNA. What about cereal?
Max?

(**MAX** *grabs his phone and starts dialing a cab.*)

MAX. What?

ANNA. I want to eat cereal with you.

MAX. I know, but we don't have – *(on the phone)* yeah, hi, we need a pickup to the airport, to JFK? 917-345-6779. Yeah, same address. Like as soon as you humanly can get here. Like now.

ANNA. *(starts to cry)* I don't even have my toiletries ready.

MAX.	**ANNA.**
(still on the phone)	You can't ship me
Thank you.	toiletries.

MAX. Just get yourself ready, OK? He's coming in like ten.

ANNA. Who's coming?

MAX. The *cab*, the cab is coming in ten minutes, OK, so you gotta –

ANNA. I'm not ready to go, though. I'm not ready, I'm not even –

MAX. I know! So just start getting stuff together, come on.

> (**ANNA** *moves very slowly to her suitcase and zips it up.)*
>
> *(She's crying now.)*

OK, sorry Scoot, you gotta – we gotta move this along a little bit.

ANNA. I don't want to go.

MAX. What do you mean you don't / wanna go –

ANNA. I don't want to go, I'm not ready.

MAX. You have to be ready, you have to be –

ANNA. I'm not ready at all.

MAX. Yeah, you are, you just overslept, it's fine, we'll make it –

ANNA. I know, but I'm not, I'm not ready –

> *(She falls into him, sobbing.)*

MAX. No.

No, what is this? Come on, you can't – don't.
Don't do this.
I'm awake, I'm here to say *goodbye*, it's 5:30 in the fucking morning and – God, you don't even have any

of your stuff ready, you've had six months to pack for this, Anna –

ANNA. *(small)* Come here…

MAX. No, NO, I can't *deal* with this, you *want* this, this is what you wanted, so –

>*(super positive again)*

Let's go! OK? Come on, Ann! You need to go.

>*(He starts trying to put on her shoes, but she's not helping.)*

ANNA. I made a mistake, let's just figure it out, we can figure it out.

MAX. We will, OK, we'll be fine, but come on! We need to go now, Ann.

ANNA. I love you so much.

MAX. Come on.

ANNA. I made a mistake.

MAX. Scooter, come on. Let's go. Come on, Anna.

>*(He tries to move her.)*

Let's go.

>*(He tries to move her again, but she stays there, all her weight on **MAX**, leaning against her half-stuffed suitcase on the ground.)*

>*(Finally, they get up and move to the door.)*

>*(They stand in the doorway.)*

>*(They say goodbye.)*

>*(The light is blinding.)*

>*(A sound cue builds, and then breaks.)*

TWENTY FOUR

Long Distance Call (And One Call From Long Ago) Montage

(MAX and ANNA move throughout the stage.)

(They're on cell phones.)

ANNA. But if I stay in this Gender in Cinema class then I'll have to add like two extra credits over the next few years –

MAX. Oh, really?

ANNA. Yeah, so, I mean, to *me* it doesn't make much sense to stay in it just cause I *like* it, you know?

MAX. Yeah.

ANNA. Like I can't really be doing stuff like that, I should be thinking about practicality and money and / all that stuff –

MAX. Yeah, I mean – / That's –

ANNA. But Handley – I mean Handley said it made sense to take whatever I want in my first year, / 'cause it's still –

MAX. Who said?

(MAX grabs a bag of chips. Starts eating them.)

ANNA. Handley, my advisor.

MAX. Oh yeah.

ANNA. But I don't want to stress out about having to take up too many credits when I'm trying to do my thesis, you know?

...

Are you eating?

MAX. No.

ANNA. Yes, you are. You're eating chips.

MAX. I'm not.

ANNA. You're not even trying to hide the crunching.

> *(shift)*

> *(Another call.)*

MAX. How much did you say for the end of October?

ANNA. Um, last ones I saw were like four hundred fifty dollars –

MAX. Shit, what did you use?

ANNA. I checked a bunch of the sites –

MAX. Well, can we still do Thanksgiving somewhere? My mom would love to have you.

ANNA. Shit, my parents bought me my ticket home already. Can you come to my house?

MAX. No, no, Scoot, 'cause this is the first Thanksgiving my mom's –

ANNA.	**MAX.**
Oh, yeah, yeah, of course.	I gotta…

ANNA. I just… Damn.

> *(shift)*

> *(Another call.)*

> *(loud bar music plays)*

ANNA. *(yelling over the music)* HEYYY!

MAX. Hey, I can't hear you/ like at all –

ANNA. YEAH I'M LIKE HIDING IN THE CORNER OF THIS BAR –

MAX. Can you just step outside a sec?

ANNA. NO IF I LEAVE I CAN'T GO BACK INSIDE, THEY'RE REALLY INTENSE ABOUT IT.

MAX.	**ANNA.**
Ah, OK, well.	Happy New Year!
Happy New Year.	

MAX. Who are / you with?

ANNA. I'm at a bar!

MAX. WHO ARE YOU HANGING OUT WITH?

ANNA. IT'S A BAR IN SANTA MONICA CALLED
PENGUINS.

>   *(Offstage, people cheer.)*

HAPPY NEW YEAR!!

MAX. Who are / you with?

ANNA. SORRY, WHAT?

MAX. WHO ARE YOU HANGING / OUT WITH?

ANNA. IT'S CALLED PENGUINS.

MAX. OK, this is –

ANNA. LOVE / YOU, SCOOTER!

MAX. Love you.

>   *(shift)*

>   *(Another call.)*

>   (**MAX** *pulls a box out, and digs through it.*)

ANNA. I guess I just don't understand what's in it.

MAX. I don't know either, it's a bunch of crap, but it's been
sitting in the closet since you left and I either want to
ship it or throw it away.

ANNA. What's – can you just tell me what's in it?

>   *(He dumps the contents of the box onto the ground.)*

>   *(And everything spills out.)*

>   *(Boggle, the climate conference key chains, the
>   Jellyfish brochure, the dreamcatcher, the scented
>   candle.)*

>   *(They all tumble out.)*

MAX. Just like – a bunch of stuff.

>   *(He goes through it piece by piece.)*

ANNA. If I feel like I'm missing anything that I really need
I'll let you know.

MAX. It's your stuff, though.

ANNA. Well, it's yours now. You're keeping it warm for me.

MAX. You should probably come over to my house and take a look.

ANNA. You should come over to my house and bring it with you.

MAX. Well, as soon as you have a free fucking *week*end, I will.

ANNA. OK, look, just, you know, hang on to it or throw it out, it's whatever.

MAX. Well, which?

ANNA. I don't…

Just do whatever.

>   *(shift)*

>   *(Another call.)*

>   (**JAY** *appears in low light.*)

>   (**AVERY** *sits on the bed, while* **MAX** *talks on the phone.*)

>   (*All four of them are spread out, they speak quickly.*)

It wasn't for any reason, I just had a really late screening –

MAX. How come I can pick up the phone whenever and it's like fucking impossible to get you on the phone at night –

JAY. This is my ninth call in the last couple weeks, where are ya? What are you doing?

AVERY. Do you want wine or beer?

JAY. I have the best deal for you for the summer, OK, you're gonna love it.

AVERY. Can we not fuckin' stay in and sulk tonight? Let's go out somewhere! We can go eat cupcakes, / I don't care what we do –

MAX. *(to* **ANNA***)* Can you just try – can we get some kind of routine together? I'll make us a calendar or something.

JAY. A month in Argentina, you'll get free room and board in this incredible house, you just have to shoot during the day, so you have all the nights free to do whatever –

ANNA. You said you didn't want to do that.

MAX. I know, but it makes me picture like seventeen million dicks inside you.

ANNA. Jesus Christ, / Max, come on.

JAY. I want you to get on this trip so you have to call me back, OK?

ANNA. I have stuff I'm doing, Max. / I do stuff here.

AVERY. I came all the way from *Queens.*

MAX. I'm not asking you to be on *call.*

ANNA. Then, what are you asking?

MAX. For you to *want* to answer the phone when I call you.

ANNA. I can't if I'm fucking *busy,* Max!

MAX. Wow.

JAY. You've gotta call me back, though, OK?

Just call me back and we'll just talk about it.

MAX. You're being crazy.

ANNA. I can't – I gotta go.

> *(shift)*

> *(Another call.)*

> *(**MAX** takes his guitar, moves to center stage.)*

> *(He's all nerves and smiles.)*

> *(**AVERY**, **JAY**, and **ANNA** watch him in dusted light.)*

> *(**MAX** starts to play a song.)*

> *(The following is played as overlapping, recorded dialogue.)*

> *(It crescendos, voice on voice on voice, as **MAX**'s guitar playing builds…)*

MAX. So I just played a show! I played a *gig.* I came and I sat there on the little stool and I played some songs and…

JAY. Annabelle.

ANNA. Jayface.

MAX. ...it was a fuckin' *disaster*, / Anna. It was the most embarrassing experience I think I've ever had, you know? / I forgot my tuner so the whole thing was like slightly off.

AVERY. Max, wasn't – *(into the phone)*
Anna, it wasn't that bad, he's being dramatic.

JAY. I'm coming to your screening.

ANNA. What? No way, you're flying in for it?

MAX. Crowd banter is really hard, I think I talked about ninjas for at least three minutes –

JAY. Yeah, I have like a week off between now and Warsaw, so I figured I'd come eat fish tacos / and hang out.

AVERY. I think your exact words were, "Ninjas would really like this one 'cause it kind of, you know, it kind of sneaks up on you."

ANNA. You'll love everybody here, man, they're all weird and smarter than me and international.

MAX. Avery's making it sound like it was funny, but it was more sad / than funny, I'm pretty sure.

JAY. I want to meet the German guy.

ANNA. Which one? There's / two German guys. They're twins.

MAX. I don't know why you thought I could do this.

AVERY. Dude, calm down, let's go get – *(to ANNA on the phone)* we're gonna go get some beers,

ANNA. You love the internationals – oh man! I'm so excited you're coming, / it means so much.

JAY. *(in dark Ian McKellan voice)* I will entertain you for a period of time.

AVERY. *(to MAX)* it won't be a big deal tomorrow, OK? Come on.

ANNA. *(in same voice)* Thoroughly, I will enjoy that notion.

MAX. Anyway, this message is too long...
I guess you're editing, or...

JAY. You gonna give a speech?

ANNA. I might. *(laughs)* I might give a speech.

MAX. I don't know where you are

I don't know your schedule or what you're doing and you don't feel the need to tell me, because…you know, I don't know where you are in the morning or at night or on the weekends, I don't know where you are right now, I have no / idea what you're doing.

AVERY. Max, come on – let's hang up now. 'Night, Anna!

       (**AVERY** *and* **JAY** *are bathed in darkness.*)

       (*a long silence*)

       (*Another call.*)

ANNA. OK.

MAX. I told you so you'd be jealous, I wanted to make you jealous.

ANNA. I mean, did you like it?

MAX. No.

ANNA. Was it in our bed?

   **

Let's just be honest, you know?
We haven't been able to see each other since Thanksgiving, it's too hard.
I kissed someone.

MAX. You told me.

ANNA. Just some guy.
Definitely wasn't the girl I always…

       (**ANNA** *stifles tears.*)

MAX. I love you so *much*, for fuck's sake, you're the only thing I ever…
Just let me back in there, OK?
Please.

ANNA. I can't.

MAX. Just do it. You just open yourself back up and let me back in there, OK, that's what you do. It's easy.

ANNA. No.

>   *(short beat)*

We were a time in each other's lives, you know?

I think that's…we were just a chunk of time.

MAX. Just. Let me fly out there. Let me do something.

ANNA. I don't think so.

MAX. *(pleading)* Why?

ANNA. Because I know.

I think I know, so it's not worth…

I like it here.

I'm happy.

I like the sun.

MAX. So do I.

I like the sun.

ANNA. No, it's…

…

I don't need you anymore.

MAX. You never wanted to need me.

ANNA. I know, but now I just…

I mean now it's all…

It's just all muffled, I think, and it's too… It's…

>   *(The lights shift, gradually exploding into*
>   *something bright, beautiful, sunny.* MAX *takes his*
>   *phone, and feverishly dials* ANNA.*)*

>   *(Another call.)*

MAX. Heyyyyyy.

ANNA. Hey, who is this?

MAX. Oh, sorry, it's Max. That guy Max you met.

ANNA. Oh from the –

MAX. Yeah, you gave me your number!

ANNA. I know. How's it goin'?

MAX. It's good. It's awesome.

You gave me your real number!

ANNA. Yeah, why wouldn't I?

MAX. I just didn't know if you'd…

Oh, shit. Do you hear – shit, do you have a delay on your phone?

ANNA. Nope.

MAX. *(talking weird because of the delay)* It's – it's like making all my words come after I'm speaking them. It's like the –

Ahhhhhh, this is… / ah, sorry.

ANNA. It's OK. Do you want to call me back real quick?

MAX. No, I'm gonna suck this up and deal with it.

ANNA. You can call me back, it's OK.

MAX. No! It's all good, it totally just stopped, it's gone. But hey I think we should go out and see a movie or go to dinner or both.

> *(He takes out a bag of chips and starts eating them.)*

ANNA. Yeah, totally, I'd love to.

MAX. Awesome.

ANNA. Yeah, I can probably do something on –

> *(She laughs.)*

Are you…

Are you eating?

MAX. What?

ANNA. You're eating something.

MAX. Oh, yeah I'm eating chips.

ANNA. That's – is that something you do on the phone?

> *(ANNA moves slowly into the apartment.)*

> *(And now she's there.)*

MAX. I'll give you one if you want.

> *(ANNA stands next to MAX who splays out on the couch.)*

> *(They look at each other…)*

TWENTY-FIVE

(It's the night they met.)

(ANNA paces around, uncomfortable at first, taking her time easing into things.)

ANNA. No, thanks, I'm good.

MAX. Are you sure?

ANNA. Yeah.

MAX. They're good chips. Baked. They're Baked Lays.

ANNA.	MAX.
I can see that.	Healthier.

(ANNA stands.)

ANNA. Oh man, I can't believe Allie ditched me.

MAX. It's pretty late.

ANNA. Yeah. Did you see them leave? Ryan and Allie and those guys?

MAX. Mmhm, I watched them leave.

ANNA. Did they say where they were going?

MAX. Yeah, they said the train.

(beat)

MAX. Who are you?

ANNA. Oh, I'm Anna – I came with Allie, we went to school together.

(MAX stands, too.)

MAX. Do you want a glass of wine?

ANNA. No, I'm good, I had a bunch to drink earlier.

MAX. Sames.
We had a lot of fun here tonight.

ANNA. Yeah, sorry I missed so much of it, I got here real late, so –

MAX. Best night of my life.

ANNA. Well, I'm sad I missed it.

(She checks her phone.)

ANNA. Shit.

MAX. No drink, really? You sure? I have a lovely *Shiraz.*

ANNA. No, it's late.

MAX. It's lovely.

A lovely Shiraz.

ANNA. Thanks, I'm good.

MAX. Howbout some apple sauce?

ANNA. What?

MAX. For some reason I have a shitload of apple sauce in my refrigerator I think cause my friend came over and made a bunch of Potato Latkes *(pronounces it: Late-kees)*

ANNA. I think it's Laht-kuzz.

MAX. No, it's Late-keez.

ANNA. Oh, I see. Hey, can I – do you have a number for a cab company?

MAX. Oh, yeah, sure. Let me look here.

> *(He takes out his phone, goes to the couch. Scrolls a bit.)*

Do you want to see some of my photo gallery?

ANNA. No, I'm good.

MAX. Do you want to see some of my apps?

ANNA. No, just the cab is good.

> *(***MAX*** dials, then waits a moment.)*

MAX. Hi, this is Max Storrs from the Storrs family, we need a pick-up at 15th and Prospect.

Going to…

ANNA. Classon / and Fulton.

MAX. Clapton and… Fulman.

ANNA. Classon and Fulton.

MAX. Clamafultion.

ANNA. *(taking the phone from him)* Hi, yeah, I'm sorry, um, it's *Classon* and *Fulton.*

MAX. That's what I said.

ANNA. *(to phone)* Thank you.

(She hands the phone back to **MAX**.*)*

(a moment of silence)

*(***ANNA*** checks her phone again.)*

ANNA. Shit, I have to wake up in like four hours.

MAX. For what?

ANNA. For work.

MAX. What's work on a Saturday?

ANNA. I P.A.

MAX. Beer.

ANNA. What?

MAX. I.P.A. It's a beer type.

ANNA. *(amused)* No, I P.A. Like for movies.

MAX. You pick apples for movies.

ANNA. Oh, wow, you're full of wordy games –

MAX. I love them.

ANNA. Very cool.

MAX. Do you want to sit on the couch now?

ANNA. Do I what?

MAX. Do you want to just – you can just sit now?

ANNA. You want me to sit with you?

MAX. I just think we can sit together while you wait for your transportation.

Plus I'll…draw you. If you sit here.

ANNA. You'll *draw* me? What does that mean?

MAX. It means I want to draw you. If you sit here I'll draw you.

I'm really good at drawing.

> *(She sits on the couch with him, leaving a big space between them.)*

That is perfect placement.

ANNA. OK, go ahead.

MAX. I have to look at you for a bit.

> *(He does.)*

I really love all of your face.

ANNA. Hey, thanks.

MAX. Your hair is also great.

ANNA. You need paper.

MAX. I *know.*

> *(He gets up and goes to his printer and gets a piece of paper.)*

> *(He grabs a green pencil from a drawer in the desk.)*

ANNA. I thought you were an artist or something.

MAX. I am.

ANNA. You're using printer paper.

MAX. That's my thing.

ANNA. Uh huh.

MAX. No, you'll see, I'm really good at this. I'm like Picasso mixed with the – other painters.

> *(**MAX** sits back down.)*

> *(He starts to draw.)*

Could you arrange yourself in a way that is comfortable please?

> *(She adjusts, slightly.)*

Mmhm. Stay there.

ANNA. You're using a green pencil.

MAX. Yes.

ANNA. Do I look green to you?

MAX. *(artist-serious)* Very much, yes.

ANNA. It's not just some arbitrary color you found in your desk?

MAX. No, I saw you and immediately thought: green. Green outline.

ANNA. I think it's just 'cause you don't have any other pencils.

**

MAX. *(slowly, as he continues to draw)* Someday I'm gonna give this to you.

ANNA. Oh yeah? Some day?

MAX. Mmhm.

I'm gonna find you and give this to you and it'll be worth so much money because I'll be this very successful drawer – draw-*ist* – and you'll look at it and just be like, "Wow, Max Storrs drew me better than anyone in the world, he just – he looked at me *once*, like one time, and he got the whole of me onto a piece of paper with this one, green colored pencil," and you'll be totally *floored* because it is just spot. On. I mean, "This is really good," you'll say. And we'll go ahead and sell the drawing in an auction or another place and you'll kiss me and we'll get married and adopt a gaggle of Romanian children.

ANNA. Jesus. A gaggle?

> *(**MAX** nods.)*

MAX. And in three years you're going to break my heart into a thousand pieces.

> *(beat)*

But it'll all be worth it.

ANNA. Yeah?

MAX. I think so.

> *(He draws.)*
>
> *(a moment)*
>
> *(Then he looks up.)*

OK.

It's done.

> *(He looks at her for a long time.)*

It's you.

> *(blackout)*

End of Play

Lightning Source UK Ltd.
Milton Keynes UK
UKOW06f0157070416

271749UK00006B/82/P

9 780573 704604